COMINGS AND GOINGS

Originally from Galway, Grainne Toher works in banking in Dublin.

She took on writing to pass the time while commuting to and from work.

This is her first novel.

COMINGS AND GOINGS

Grainne Toher

COMINGS AND GOINGS

Olympia Publishers
London

www.olympiapublishers.com
OLYMPIA PAPERBACK EDITION

Copyright © Grainne Toher 2010

The right of Grainne Toher to be identified as author of
this work has been asserted in accordance with sections 77 and 78 of
the Copyright, Designs and Patents Act 1988.

All Rights Reserved

No reproduction, copy or transmission of this publication
may be made without written permission.
No paragraph of this publication may be reproduced,
copied or transmitted save with the written permission of the publisher,
or in accordance with the provisions
of the Copyright Act 1956 (as amended).

Any person who commits any unauthorised act in relation to
this publication may be liable to criminal
prosecution and civil claims for damage.

A CIP catalogue record for this title is
available from the British Library.

ISBN: 978-1-84897-086-1

This is a work of fiction.
Names, characters, places and incidents originate from the writer's
imagination. Any resemblance to actual persons, living or dead, is
purely coincidental.

First Published in 2010

Olympia Publishers
60 Cannon Street
London
EC4N 6NP

Printed in Great Britain

Acknowledgements

To my Dad, Jim Toher (RIP), my first editor who enjoyed the read even though 'it wasn't his genre' .

To my Mum, Mary Toher, who kindly fixed up my grammar and threw in some helpful suggestions.

To my husband Michael, for encouraging me to keep at it.

To my good friends, for saying they enjoyed the first few chapters and that they wanted to read the rest of it.

Contents

Chapter 1 **The Keys**	15
Chapter 2 **The Girls**	19
Chapter 3 **Anne**	27
Chapter 4 **John**	33
Chapter 5 **Apartment**	39
Chapter 6 **Timmy**	45
Chapter 7 **Mum**	51
Chapter 8 **Ger**	61
Chapter 9 **Dad**	65
Chapter 10 **Paul**	69
Chapter 11 **Jeanette**	73
Chapter 12 **Paul**	79

Chapter 13 **First Date**	**83**
Chapter 14 **Jeanette**	**87**
Chapter 15 **Ger**	**91**
Chapter 16 **Farewell**	**95**
Chapter 17 **Paul**	**101**
Chapter 18 **John**	**105**
Chapter 19 **Dad**	**107**
Chapter 20 **John**	**111**
Chapter 21 **The Real World**	**119**
Chapter 22 **Pam**	**123**
Chapter 23 **Berlin**	**125**
Chapter 24 **New Arrival**	**131**
Chapter 25 **The Girls**	**133**

Chapter 1

The Keys

Marise hugged herself with glee. Imagine, thirty-eight-years-old and only now did she own her own home. She had just collected the keys to her two-bed pied á terre in the leafy suburb of Ranelagh in Dublin's Southside. Thank God for the recession. A few years ago she would have to buy in the Northside at these prices. In actual fact, she had owned a home before, but with a cheating fiancé who couldn't keep his hands to himself in the kitchen at dinner parties. But no, this one was all her own and no-one else was going to get the key, ever! After what she had been through with the overly tactile ex-fiancé, her heart was locked for keeps as well.

*****

Marise was so looking forward to decorating the place exactly as she wanted – all cream walls and dark furniture, soft lighting and wooden floors. She would look into landscaping the tiny handkerchief lawn at the back to make it as low maintenance as possible; no muss, no fuss and absolutely no cats.

*****

Her job as an ad-agency manager frequently took her off to London and New York. She loved taking a brief or a concept and thrashing it out in a boardroom with her team. It thrilled her to bounce ideas around for hours on end, sometimes into the wee hours and come up with a campaign. Her recent successful campaigns were for Million Dollar Babes fashion road shows and a slick, award-winning mobile phone television advert.

*****

Marise popped into the crumbling shower of her old apartment. She was fond of the place. It had been her haven after the broken engagement, but she was glad to be moving out this Sunday to start a new chapter. Besides it was close to falling in.

Chapter 2

The Girls

She got ready for celebratory drinks with the gang later in town. The gang had met while flipping burgers at Supermacs during college and had remained close friends ever since. Jeanette, who was a GP, was married to Mick, who had made burgers with them too. They had two small children, Jack and Kayleigh. She was dying to get out of the house for some adult conversation. Pam, their pal, was joining them. She was a teacher and was married to Joe for six years. She and her husband had grown tired of waiting for Mother Nature to take her course and were applying for foreign adoption.

*****

Timmy, who used to serve up their cocktails in the pub after they finished their shifts in Supermacs, was joining them too. Timmy was now a civil servant and their token gay best friend and fashionista. He would undoubtedly appraise their hair, clothes and make-up, generally keep them fashion forward and bitch about their other friends.

*****

They were going to start the evening in that new place off Stephen's Green and take it from there. Marise, nicely tanned from a recent trip to Spain, donned her black Diane von Furstenburg wrap dress with some strappy sandals. Thankfully, she needed minimal make-up due to her sun-kissed glow; just a touch of blush, gloss and mascara. She looked nothing like her thirty-eight years and could pass for about thirty-two in soft lighting.

*****

Jeanette, a petite blonde, was first to arrive, having escaped two screaming kids, one a new born, pawning them off on her unfortunate, worn out husband. She was wearing an aquamarine figure hugging top with black cigarette pants.

"God," said Marise hugging her, "how did you lose the baby weight so quickly?"

"Well when I read in the celebrity gossip magazines that people lost weight running around after two small children, I used to scoff but it's true. Besides I forget to graze like I used to. I haven't the time anyway," said Jeanette.

"By the way, congratulations on the new place. When's the house warming?"

"Well I have to get in first," said Marise, "but I'm definitely planning something. I'll keep you posted."

*****

They spotted Pam making her way towards them, looking fabulous as usual, with not a line on her face. She gets a full night's sleep, thought Jeanette, hugging her.

Pam had her own troubles, but tonight she was celebrating. She and Joe had passed the preliminary stages of the Adoption assessment and were due to start the Adoption course and home study anytime soon. She was on for a good night out away from the drama and heartache of it all. Pam was godmother to Jeanette's oldest, Jack, and she adored him.

*****

"Marise, now that you have your own place, the guy of your dreams will just appear. You know that's the way it works, the zen of archery or something. I read about it," said Pam.

"Well, I hope he takes his time. I'm enjoying my space and my life way too much for some guy to come along and spoil it all now," said Marise.

Marise had dated most of Joe and Mick's single guy friends at this stage. Nothing had come of any of the dates and Marise was starting to feel paranoid and predatory when she met the guy's friends at this stage.

"The right one doesn't spoil everything," said Pam, who despite the stress of the baby stuff was still head over heels with Joe.

"OK, Mrs Mills and Boon, enough of all that romantic nonsense. I'll get the drinks in. Same again everyone?"

Pam and Jeanette exchanged smiles. They wanted someone great for Marise, who was a great pal to them both.

*****

In walked Timmy, late and flamboyant, blowing air-kisses to everyone he knew. It took him a while to reach their table. Somehow or other he had managed to get himself into a rubber top and pants, something to do with talcum powder. Anyway, it was too much information. As usual, he regaled them with stories of his sexploits and protracted one-night stands, both shocking and hilarious. Deep down, the girls knew that like everyone else, he was looking for love. Jeanette rejoined with a few stories of her own about some of her young male patients and their odd assortment of ailments from the bizarre to the ridiculous.

"They just fancy you," said Marise.

Jeanette wasn't so sure. It was endearing, thought Marise, that she had no idea how gorgeous she was.

A couple of drunken guys made their way over to the table to chat them up, asking them how they all knew each other.

"I bet ye made lovely burgers together," said one lasciviously staring at Pam and Jeanette's ample chests.

"Yes," continued Jeanette innocently. "Pam used to toast the buns and I used to…"

"Ignore them," laughed Marise. "They're ossified."

Many cocktails later, the gang headed for the obligatory dirty bag of chips and joined the queue for the taxi home.

Chapter 3

Anne

Marise groped around for the ringing phone, a little too early one morning. It was Anne, her little sister. She wanted to meet up. She wouldn't talk over the telephone. She sounded anxious. Marise was anxious now too. She hoped all was OK with Dad. She worried about how he was coping without Mum and was constantly trying to come up with ways to entertain and interest him. They were all quite close since Mum passed away. Marise and Anne agreed to meet up for supper that evening in Bewley's on Grafton Street to talk. Anne was the surprise baby who had come along while Marise and Declan were in their teens. She was still the baby and the apple of Dad's eye, the source of most of the family drama. She got away with murder. Marise and Declan had paved the way for an easier life for their younger sibling. Declan was in Australia. He had moved about a year after Mum died. He was a builder by trade and couldn't find work in Ireland anymore. Marise felt that he wanted to get away to sort out his head with Mum gone. He was her pet.

*****

Marise found the will to pack up her boxes for the very last time, and wondered what was Anne's news.

*****

Anne cut a defiant but vulnerable figure in the

back of Bewleys. The stained-glass windows provided a pleasant backdrop. Like your typical teenager these days, her eye make-up was overdone (probably blagged at the BT's Mac counter), her hair was straightened, she wore a denim skirt, ski-pants, ugg boots and the all important eight hundred euros worth of handbag on her arm, probably a present from over-compensating Dad.

Anne stared up at Marise balefully with her big brown eyes.

"I'm pregnant," she mumbled.

"You're what?" exclaimed Marise. "Who's the guy? I thought you were single!"

"I am now," sighed Anne mournfully.

"What the heck happened, apart from the obvious? I know how 'that' happens," joked Marise but stopped herself when she saw Anne's expression.

"Well, don't get mad at me... we were only together a few months... I thought it was serious... he said he was single... then I got a phone-call from this crazy woman yelling 'Stay away from my husband you home-wrecker...' I nearly died... I had no idea," sobbed Anne.

"What did you say to her?" asked Marise.

"I hung up the phone. What could I say? I haven't heard from either of them since. That was a few weeks ago. He hasn't called. He mustn't have loved me after all..." wailed Anne.

"Lucky escape I'd say. Stay away from them, you hear me?" said Marise.

"I don't feel lucky. I loved him and I thought he loved me," said Anne.

"Love me eye," said Marise.

Anne could be so gullible sometimes. Your man was obviously not getting it at home with a wife who didn't understand him. She hoped Anne would stay away and have some sense.

"I'll be giving him a call for money for the operation. If he says no, I'll tell his wife I'm pregnant," said Anne.

"Operation, surely not that, in this day and age with all the other options open to you nowadays," exclaimed Marise, her heart sinking thinking of childless Pam.

"My mind is made up and, anyway, you're not my mother," said Anne, her voice rising tremulously a fraction at the end. They both missed Mum right now.

Marise was in no mood to argue. In her little world away from the family, life was good. Her new apartment was great and she adored her friends. She wanted to hold that good feeling. Besides, Anne was a big girl now.

Anne liked to act the tough, defiant teenager but Marise knew that she was a total softie underneath. For now, the pair decided to keep things to themselves and spare Dad any worry.

"Promise me you'll come with me to London and hold my hand?" said Anne.

Marise said she'd think about it. She had mixed

feelings about it on many levels.

"For now, promise me you'll go to the doctor for a check-up to make sure you are both OK?" countered Marise.

"I promise," agreed Anne grudgingly.

Marise gratefully fled back to her packing. Sisters, who'd have them?

Chapter 4

John

Good old reliable John. Her old pal John showed up to help with the move first thing next day. You could set your clock by him. She couldn't help noticing how well he looked. He was beaming and seemed to have trimmed down a bit.

She and John had had a few drunken snogs over the years, but nothing had ever come of it. She knew John from across the road since they were both in nappies. They often climbed trees together as children. In recent years he had gotten a bit fond of the sauce so she had taken a step back from him. He came out with mad, strange stuff when he was under the influence. He was sober now though and although very cute, he was a bit too quiet for mad Marise as she had been nicknamed in college. Besides, if he hadn't the bottle to ask her out after the snogs, he was probably a little bit quiet in the bedroom, too. Her ideal man needed a bit of oomph to fit in with her busy lifestyle and personality. Right now though, she felt very comforted by the fact that he was here with her. Being from the same road, he had always been around for those seminal moments in her life, her graduation, her Mum's passing and that awful break-up. All the hard stuff really.

The packing was done. She was just finishing scrubbing the place. Although crumbling, she couldn't bear to leave a messy flat for someone else to walk into. Dropping the key to the flat into the mailbox, they loaded up their respective vehicles and headed for Ranelagh.

*****

Once in the new apartment, Marise fished out the kettle, hob-nobs, tea and milk. She'd keep the champagne for when the girls came around.

"What do you think of it?" she asked.

"It's fabulous Marise, fair play to you," said John.

"Well, I'm glad you are here for my very first cup of tea," she said.

"Marise, I've met someone," said John.

"Oh, that's nice," said Marise, too brightly.

She was trying to sound light but her tone betrayed her. What the hell was wrong with her? Was she jealous? Surely not.

"I really, really like her," said John.

"What does she do?" asked Marise.

"She's a vet. She looked after Rusty when he was sick. She was so good with him, I fell for her."

Marise knew with a sinking feeling that this was the way to John's heart. She couldn't bear animals – all that mess.

"Well, I'm happy for you," lied Marise. "Its time you met someone."

"She's only twenty-five, but she is so mature," said John.

He was smitten. She let him rattle on. She tried to hide the fact that she felt like she had just been stung by a bee. She said, "Isn't that lovely. I must have you both over so that I can meet her." She had no intention of it.

Obliviously, John finished up his tea and headed off. He had a date with the lovely twenty-five-year-old Laura.

Marise started to empty boxes and place things around her apartment, but was annoyingly distracted by John's news. She felt like she had been hit by a train. It wouldn't last. Laura was too young. He needed someone more mature. Twenty-five indeed!

Fishing out a mirror from one of the boxes, she hung it up and examined her eyes for crow's feet. She made a mental note to book herself in for an eyebrow tint and wax in the morning.

She took another look around and started to feel excited again about the possibilities of the new apartment. It was a new phase in her life and she was going to enjoy it. Everyone else was getting on with their lives and she resolved to do the same…

Chapter 5

Apartment

Marise gazed dreamily out the office window. The sun was shining and she was perishing under the air-con vent. She was wrapped in a pashmina for God's sake. What was up with that? She could see the canal from her office and made a mental note to drop into that funky new 'Mobl' furniture place off Leeson Street, to see if she could spot some unusual pieces for the apartment. She liked to feel cutting edge – ahead of the posse. She often was.

*****

On Friday she and the girls had arranged a painting party. The paint was bought, mostly magnolia, with the odd red wall here and there. Afterwards, they were going to sit around, eat Chinese, bitch about work, men and drink a bottle of champagne. Marise had had a few dates recently, nothing serious. In fact, a girl in work had mentioned this new dating outfit called 'It's Just Dinner' and they were going to give it a bash together. At the back of her mind was John.

She wondered what the lovely Laura was really like. John was a lovely guy. She'd better not break his heart this Laura one.

*****

She had arranged to meet Anne after work and she

was not looking forward to it. By now, Anne was six weeks gone and talking about the trip to London. Marise dreaded this thought but as the nearest thing to a mother Anne had, she was trying to offer unbiased support.

Marise looked up at the clock. It was half three. She had barely done a stroke today. Things had been so quiet everywhere since the recession had hit. Everyone was watching their advertising budgets. This week she had been tasked with giving marketing and advertising training sessions to client's staff to pass the time. They were on the doss big-time. She reckoned, if things didn't pick up, they would all be in New Zealand or Canada this time next year or signing on with the rest of them.

For her own part, ever-resourceful Marise knew she would be fine. She still had her first communion money, a fact that she kept to herself. She always had a plan or a project, so much so that her personal life was loaded with responsibility and projects. She often struggled to lighten the heck up and enjoy herself.

Marise pulled into her very own parking space in the apartment complex. She got that familiar thrilled feeling. It's all mine, she thought. Grabbing her cool retro lamp and funky shaped chair, she turned the key in the door. She was glad to be home.

*****

She had met Anne who had been hormonal and emotional. Anne had talked about phoning the baby's father to plead with him to see her. Marise had dissuaded her this time, but wasn't sure she wouldn't call him eventually.

Marise grabbed an old Bruce Springsteen CD off the rack, put it on the deck and danced around the kitchen with the mop, belting along with the words to 'Dancing in the Dark'. She was happy alone, but now and then, she thought it would be nice to have someone just for a Saturday night and Sunday afternoon.

She was meeting Timmy for lunch tomorrow and couldn't wait. He always made her laugh. He was a hoot.

Chapter 6

Timmy

Marise hooked up with Timmy at Café Bar Deli off George's Street. He had on his sparkly eyeliner, winkle pickers and a batwing top.

Air-kissing her. "Oh Marise, I've really blown it this time." he smirked.

"What now?" she asked.

"Well, I got banged up in the cop shop overnight last week." Just how many double entendres can one sentence have, she wondered.

"Tell me more," she said.

"I was done for lewd conduct. I'm so embarrassed."

"Poor you." said Marise playing along, knowing he was loving the drama.

Timmy's folks had disowned him long ago. This latest revelation wouldn't help matters.

"Well, the incident was in the papers. Word has got out that it was me."

"How did word get out Timmy?" asked Marise, patiently.

"Well, I might have mentioned it in passing to someone I thought I could trust at work."

"Show me the paper," said Marise. He handed it to her. "I bet you will frame this, you devil."

Marise wondered how he had lasted in the civil service for so long. They had been turning a blind eye to his shenanigans for a while but this was over the top. In the current climate they were probably looking for excuses to get rid of people. This kind of stuff would bump him right up the list.

"So what will you do?"

"Well I'm way too mortified to go back. I went in last Monday and got propositioned by several fuglies I've worked alongside for years, and that I have never spoken to before. Hideous," he groaned. "I'm going to apply for a severance package. I've been there for years. It should be worth my while I reckon."

"You'll never find anything else at the moment," said Marise.

"I have a plan," said Timmy. "An old friend has moved to Berlin. He is setting up his own bakery called 'Kaiser Konditorei' – and wants me to go in with him."

"That's right up your alley. What if they don't accept you for a severance package?" asked Marise.

"Oh, I think they will," said Tim.

"Well, there are worse people than you going

around at the minute," said Marise, "think of all the politicians and property developers who had practically hung the country out to dry. Your antics will be forgotten soon." said Marise.

"OK, OK, let's not go there. I'm so tired of listening to the doom and gloom these days. Everyone is suddenly an expert on the economy just because they are paying more taxes and their home has gone down in value. It's worse than the boom years, when all people could talk about was the value of their house – boring," said Timmy. "Let's talk about something interesting like your love life."

They both roared with laughter.

"I thought you said something interesting," said Marise. "Dublin will be a dull place without you."

"Well you'll just have to come and see me then, won't you? I'll have a nice big Kraut lined up for you. It'll put a smile back on that pinched face of yours," said Timmy.

"Bring it on, can you leave next week?" joked

Marise.

"You should really try some of that new Georgia powder from Benefit. It'd give you a bit of sparkle," said Timmy.

"Thanks a lot," said Marise. "There was me thinking I looked good. You are such a bitch, but I love you."

Chapter 7

Mum

At the painting party in Marise's apartment, three paint-speckled women in their worst gear collapsed on to a sofa covered in dustsheets.

"All done, Marise! Open the champers. Let's order the Chinese," they said in unison.

"God that was fun," said Jeanette.

"You're sad," said Marise. "You really must get out more."

"I totally agree," she nodded happily.

Her two little ones were at her Mum's for a few days and she and Mick were making the most of it. She was having fun tinged with a tiny pang of regret and had managed not to phone every hour. Tonight was their last child free night and she intended to make the most of it when she got home. The kids had to be picked up tomorrow.

Pam had been pensive all evening. Marise managed to get her on her own just after Jeanette left.

"What's up, quiet one?" asked Marise gently.

"Oh, I just wish we had our kid. I wouldn't be trying to get away," said Pam.

You're saying that now, thought Marise, but didn't say it.

"Your time will come. How is the adoption coming along?"

"Oh slowly, you know, the waiting game."

"Well, why don't you and Joe enjoy yourselves while you can? You'll have your hands full for long enough," said Marise.

"Yeah," said a deflated Pam, as she jumped into a waiting cab. No one had a clue what she was even talking about. It was taking so long.

*****

Marise went into town for a 'me' day. Since she bought the house she had eased up on the retail therapy, so she was long overdue a treat and a bit of self-gifting. She was meeting an old work pal for drinks this evening and wanted something new. Besides, the house was more or less sorted now.

She would take a quick look in Karen Millen, always a good place to start. Then she would drop into Blossom's for a facial and a pedicure, followed by a blow dry in Grant Morton's. No one else was going to look after her, so she might as well get on with it, and in the current climate it wouldn't last.

By now, she was old pals with the gang in Grant Morton and Blossoms. She bumped into them all the time in the local eateries and hot spots around town.

Marise would never forget the kindness of the lads in Grant Morton the day Mum had passed away. She was in work when she got the call – "Come quickly," said Dad. Booting her way to the hospice, she was minutes too late to say goodbye.

Not wanting to wail and scream in front of the folks, she had waited an hour or so and then needing some space to process it all, with the blood rushing past her ears, she had wandered absently towards Grant Morton.

"My Mum died," she had mumbled to Luke.

She recalled being placed gently into a chair and being minded. They refused to let her pay, if she remembers correctly. A slightly more human version of herself emerged from the salon that day. They had all been firm friends ever since.

Unable to face the hospice again, she had walked

back to the family home, picking up bread, meat slices, milk and biscuits on the way. She might as well start making sandwiches and getting the place ready for the hordes of neighbours and friends who would surely descend.

Mum had been a popular woman. She had just retired from her nursing career and was looking forward to a happy retirement with their Dad, when she was struck down with cancer. She, who had looked after others her entire life, had suffered horrendously in her last years.

Although it was going to be a relief for Mum for the pain to be over, her passing would leave an intolerable gap. As the oldest girl, Marise felt enormous pressure to fill the void. Good old John had been on the wall in front of her house when she arrived. He put out his hand.

"I'm so sorry Marise," he said. "I know how close you were. It'll take time."

Marise listened to the platitudes. He meant well.

She would hear the same ones over and over again from well-intentioned individuals who didn't know what to say, but needed to make a noise. She didn't know what to say back. She didn't want to be cruel, but thought that they hadn't a clue. They hadn't lost a parent.

"By the way, the hair looks great," said John, blushing.

That's more like it, she thought, and smiled back.

They got through the removal and burial in a daze. A serious number of people had been through the house. The women made copious pots of tea and served generous home measures of whiskey, brandy and bottles of Guinness.

The family hadn't seen some of these people for decades and knew they would not see them again until someone else died but their presence was a comfort. They seemed genuinely sorrowful for the loss of Mum. Late at night, an agitated Marise had swept furiously in and around them to get them to finish up so the family could be alone to thaw out. They seemed oblivious and lingered on.

In the weeks that followed, people told Marise to go for bereavement counselling, but she despised the idea of processing the memories a human being into a nice tidy mental file to close off. It seemed disloyal somehow. Besides, they were very open and talked about Mum a lot. They wanted to keep her memory alive. Except Declan. He stayed quiet and licked his wounds. It wasn't long after that that he had talked about emigration.

Instead of bereavement counselling, Marise decided to go to a medium, just to be different. Her Mum would have totally not approved, being a devout Catholic. Marise had to know that Mum knew that she had raced to try to make it. The medium was an unlikely bald middle-aged man called Gerry, with a hairy chest and facial hair. She was sure she could see a medallion nestling in the undergrowth on this chest. However, he was very sincere and made contact almost immediately. She knew he was genuine as he didn't ask her any questions.

"Your Mum says thanks for trying to be in two places at once, but that even you couldn't manage it," said the medium.

That sounds like her tone alright, thought Marise, suddenly feeling very comforted.

"She says she is on her way to Heaven in the company of two little angels and she is fine," said Gerry.

Mum had had a miscarriage before she had had Anne. Only Marise and her Dad knew. Marise knew who the other angel was. Marise thanked Gerry, tipped him generously and felt a major weight lift off her shoulders.

She was sitting in the chair enjoying her complimentary neck and shoulder massage, while the hair treatment soaked in and did its work.

"God, I was miles away." said Marise.

She and Luke started to chat away about their

holidays and plans for the weekend. Luke was metrosexual and gorgeous. He was very in touch with his feminine side but straight as a die. He was married to Lisa who also worked in the salon. They had a baby boy, Matthew.

Chapter 8

Ger

Marise hooked up with Ger, her old agency pal, in Moran's on Kildare Street. They had both made an effort. You never know who you might bump into. Marise looked amazing. She could feel all eyes on her but she knew in her heart she would be going alone. She never put out on a first date. He would need to be really something for her to make an exception.

Ger got the drinks in. "How's business?" she asked.

"Fine, we're ticking over," replied Marise cagily.

Everyone knew things were quiet lately.

"Our firm has let a few people go lately," said Ger. "I'm considering going out on my own."

"Are you mad?" asked Marise.

"Well, we are treating valued clients really badly as our overheads are high and they are taking the heat. They are fed up as they can see we are cutting corners and overcharging them to bring in the money," said Ger. "We have lost important clients that I've had a good relationship with for years. When things get good again, they won't touch me. I was going to ask you to come in with me," said Ger.

"Woman, I've just bought an apartment." said Marise.

"Yeah, but you bought at the right time. Your neighbours paid double what you are paying now, I bet."

She had a point.

"We could both work together and work from

home. I have state-of-the-art equipment at home, as I'm sure you do."

Marise had begun to convert her spare room into a workroom. It would be top notch.

"I could pay you top dollar as our overheads would be low. We could use hotel rooms for meetings, if needs be. Their prices are rock bottom now," continued Ger.

"Look, let me think about it," said Marise.

"You're the best in the business, Marise. Now is the time to set ourselves apart and do something different, especially when our clients need it most."

"I'll think about it alright," said Marise.

She made no major decisions without her trusty pro and con list these days. Truth be told, she had been feeling a tad disillusioned these days in work. She never told anyone this, because if she did, she would be told to be grateful to have a job. She knew in a way that they were right, but she wasn't feeling it at the moment.

"Right," said Ger, "your round, enough shop talk.

There's a bunch of hot rugby types at the bar. When you're getting the drinks in, why don't you shimmy past the one who is eyeballing you and give him a smile."

They ended up pub-crawling with the guys and dancing the night away in Leeson Street. Marise gave one of the guys, called Paul, her number. He was a rugby centre forward and a very good kisser.

Chapter 9

Dad

Marise headed over to the family home. She hadn't been there in a while. She had promised to cook the Sunday roast for Dad. She had been neglecting him a little lately, what with the apartment, Anne and everything.

Dad was a rock. She didn't know how he kept going. He and Mum had been together a really long time. He tried to be strong, cracking his old jokes, trying to be a supportive force in their lives. It was only when he went quiet that they knew he was thinking of Mum. He was lucky to have a good network of pals and his brothers close by. He had just joined the local historical society and was showing glimpses of starting to live his own life again. Marise was glad of it. It was no harm to meet a few new people. He deserved a bit of fun.

She arrived just shy of eleven o'clock and let herself in with her own key. She started to peel spuds and prepare the meat. Dad was at mass and would be home after he picked up the papers. A wraith-like Anne appeared at the kitchen door.

"You look crap," said Marise.

"Thanks sis, you always know how to make a gal feel good. Me and God just had a chat on the big white telephone."

"Tea and toast, that's what you need," said Marise.

This sent Anne running again.

"Well you're not showing yet," said Marise. "Has Dad copped anything?" she asked Anne.

"Don't think so and you'd better not say anything," said Anne.

"Don't worry," said Marise hands raised. "I'm not touching this, but he will figure it out sooner or later. Time is ticking. You need to start looking at your options."

Thank God, Declan wasn't home, He would track down the sperm donor and break his legs.

"Missie, you'll need to get some baggy T-shirts and cardigans and stuff," said Marise.

"I can borrow yours," said Anne. "You're bigger than me and I'm broke."

Broke me eye, thought Marise. Anne was tight. She'd peel an orange in her pocket that one. There was always money for handbags and visits to the hairdresser. Their Mum once said Anne would frame a shilling. They heard a key turn in the lock – Dad.

"How are my two favourite girls? What did I miss?"

"Nothing," they said in unison.

Marise glared at Anne behind Dad's back. Before she left, she made Anne promise to phone her that week with her plans.

Chapter 10

Paul

Marise had two messages on her phone when she got back. One was from Pam, asking her to call back, and the other was from Paul. Wow! She hadn't expected that. She thought she'd never see him again. She would ring him in a day or two. It was best not to look too keen. She had read 'The Rules'. She knew the drill. She rang Pam back. Pam picked up instantly.

"What's up missus?" asked Marise.

"Well, we were out for an early bird meal in Saagar last week – you know that nice Indian place I like, when we met this couple and their little Chinese baby. It was obvious they had adopted her. Well, I couldn't help myself, I went over. Joe was mortified, but he joined me eventually. We had a great old chat with them."

"I'm so glad," said Marise. "I have felt my own inadequacy in this area every time you talked to me about it. I haven't known how to help you guys. It's good you have people to talk to."

"It is. We exchanged numbers," said a delighted Pam. "We've been lone wolves for a while on this, but I feel that the tide is turning a little. We got our letter with dates for the Adoption Course today which is even better news."

"Terrific. I'm so happy for you both. You are on your way." Marise longed to spill her guts about Anne, but realised that Pam wasn't the one to do it with. Feeling duplicitous, Marise told Pam about Paul and his voicemail, adding he had a nice voice.

"That's so cool," said Pam. "Actually I bumped

into John and Laura the other day. She's nice, a little plain, a touch overweight, not really the type I thought he'd go for, but very friendly," she said treading carefully.

Pam had always thought Marise and John would end up together. She still had high hopes.

"Great, I'm going to buzz Paul back tonight," gulped Marise.

And there it was – the impetus she needed.

*****

Marise did up her pro and con list for the job with Ger. On paper, it was leaning towards going in with Ger. She would put it down for now and go back to it later, just in case. On reflection, she still had a few savings and a spare room, if the worst came to the worst, although she did love her space. She had felt a little stifled creatively lately. She reasoned that if she was going to leave a permanent and pensionable job, why not go the whole hog and set up in business herself? She could do consultancy work with Ger. This would give her the freedom to take on other projects if she needed or wanted to. She hated to be pigeon holed. She knew her own capabilities and it was true she was well-known in the industry, but she worked hard to keep it that way. Plus she wanted to feel free to look into a couple of different things like Reiki, Bio-Energy Healing, etc. She would sit down with Ger and thrash it out. She would also wait for Ger to call so as not to come across too keen. She needed to have the upper hand in negotiations if she was going to survive, pay her mortgage and have any sort of life. Ger wasn't short of a few bob.

Chapter 11

Jeanette

Just as she was dozing off, one night Marise's mobile beeped. It was a text from Anne – GOT MONEY, GOING 2 LONDON 5AM THURSDAY PLS COME. There was no word on where the money came from. Spare me the details, thought Marise. It's a good job she had annual leave left to take.

OKAY, C U AT AIRPORT. NITE was her reply to Anne's text. Cripes, thought Marise, I best get some sleep while I can.

*****

At the crack of dawn on Thursday, two cranky women met at Departures, bound for London City Airport.

"I just met him one last time to get the money. He was really nice about it. He asked whether I was OK, gave me a hug, asked did I have someone with me and stuff," said Anne.

"Grrr don't get me started," said Marise. "He doesn't want to pay maintenance, that's why he was nice. The wife would do her nut."

"Whatever," said Anne, her favourite phrase. "You hate men anyway."

"Don't start you or you'll be getting on that plane alone. It's too early to argue."

They had breakfast in silence.

Then Anne piped up, "Dad thinks I'm staying at a friend's. You won't tell him will you?"

"I'll think about it," said Marise. "Now come on brat, let's look around duty free."

Anne looked a little tearful. She was acting strong but could be such a baby herself.

*****

The clinic was all business. They dealt with people like Anne all the time. She was no big deal. The girls commenced to fill out the extensive form with its probing and personal questions. After a long wait, Anne was led away. Marise leaned back in the chair and checked her Blackberry.

Shortly after, engrossed in a spreadsheet about buyer behaviour in RI versus NI, Marise heard a little voice.

"Marise."

Looking up, there was Anne, in a blue paper gown and slippers, at the door.

"I was lying on the bed and I thought of Mum and I couldn't go through with it. I just knew she would've been so pissed off at me."

"Are you sure?" asked Marise.

"Positive," said Anne.

"Well, get your clothes on and let's get the rock out of here."

What Anne didn't know, and Marise didn't want to add to the emotionally charged moment, was that Marise had been in a similar state to Anne's one many moons ago and had gone through with it. Only Jeanette knew anything about it. It had happened just before her finals in college. She had had bouts of guilt from time to time. Following the meeting with the medium after Mum's death, she felt healed from the loss and guilt. She felt that her unborn baby might be one of the little angels who had helped Mum find her way to heaven. This consoled her greatly.

"We have four and a half hours to kill," said Marise. "Let's have a bit of lunch and get on a tour bus."

"I don't mind what we do if we stay off the London Eye. My gut is churning enough as it is," said Anne.

Over the course of the day, the two girls got misty-eyed for Mum. It always came in waves which floored you. She would've been terrific in this situation. They decided that they would tell Dad over Sunday lunch at home in a few weeks.

"Once he gets over the initial shock, I think he'll be fine," said Marise.

In fact, she was quite warming to the idea of a new baby in the house herself and playing auntie.

Chapter 12

Paul

Marise had a date with Paul that week. She had googled him and checked him out on all the social networking sites. He was squeaky clean, no hidden wives or peccadilloes that she could find. When she had called him to arrange to meet, she had blushed like a beetroot on the other end of the phone at the thought of what he might say if he knew she was running background checks on him. Well, you can't be too careful these days, she thought. Look what had happened to Anne.

She was surprised to find out how nervous she was. She felt pressurised more than usual now that the rest of her friends were coupling up. She paid a visit to the self-help or more appropriately the 'self-hell' aisle in Eason's. She didn't buy into this stuff, but needed something to occupy her. She picked up a copy of a new American book called *I Married my Best Friend*. It advocated treating every new person who came into your life as a potential friend. If the new males who came into your life became friends with benefits, then all the better, she thought.

She longed to be French. Those women were born looking airbrushed. Paul would fall in love with her instantly for her self-containment, sex appeal and innate sense of style.

Once installed in a relationship, she allowed herself to get chubby, complacent and needy. She couldn't help it. It happened. Although she leafed through the book she didn't swallow everything these so-called daytime television relationship experts said, going on with their abandonment issues and new age navel gazing crap. She'd sort herself out.

Her parents had been madly in love right up to the time Mum had taken her last breath. They were still hand holding and hugging to beat the band. As a teenager, she had been embarrassed and, now she just wanted a relationship to emulate what they had.

Cripes, she thought, listen to the trolley load of baggage I'm bringing to this date, with an almost stranger I just met in a bar. I almost feel sorry for the guy. Friends it is then, she decided.

Chapter 13

First Date

They hooked up at that swanky French restaurant off Merrion Square – L'Orage, followed by drinks in the bar of the Radisson.

The restaurant was noisy and clattery and she struggled to hear him. He, however, listened attentively and caught her every word. He was very nice, the kind of guy who opened doors for you and held out your chair. I could get used to this, she thought. He was not a typical Southside male, not the least bit arrogant and more importantly as good a kisser as she remembered. She extricated herself reluctantly from his embrace at the end of the night, but she was determined to test out the 'Friend' theory. She would make him wait and, harder still, make herself wait.

*****

She was having Ger around for lunch the next day. They were going to talk business. She had everything on paper. Ger was a tough nut to crack but then so was she.

Would she tell Ger she had met Paul?

I just said Paul, she thought.

"Paul, Paul, Paul." She grinned. It sounded nice, strong and masculine. "Paul and Marise," she said laughing.

Stop that, silenced the inner critic, you've just met.

"Shut up you," she said to no one in particular.

See co-dependent already, went the inner critic again.

"Ah, shut up," said Marise.

Giggling, she stuck on Foreigner's 'I Want to Know what Love is'. She grabbed her hairbrush as a microphone and sang her heart out.

Chapter 14

Jeanette

The phone rang. It was Jeanette.

"What's the story?" asked Marise.

"Oh you know, I'm filling out this blessed form for Pam for the adoption. The stuff they ask!"

Has the potential adoptive parent ever raised her voice in your company? I feel like saying, No, she is a robot and speaks like Stephen Hawking at all times. It gets my goat. Would you leave your children in the care of this person? I mean what the hell sort of a question is that? Of course I would. Pam is godmother to one of them for Christ's sake.

Marise realised Jeanette wasn't looking for a response from her. She merely needed to vent, so she let her. "What planet are these people from?" she continued. "Haven't they been through enough already? Pam wouldn't hurt a fly. I've seen her trap wasps under glass and set them free. Everyone else kills them. Marise are you still there?"

"I am," replied Marise.

"Sorry I'm a bit wound up," said Jeanette.

"I got that. I just think it's cool she has such a great friend in you." said Marise.

That seemed to please Jeanette.

"Two great friends," she said.

"Listen to me ranting on. How are things with you?" Marise told a little bit about Paul, not wanting to jinx it.

"Well," said Jeanette, "I have my fingers, toes and legs crossed for you."

"Jeez," said Marise, "that's a lot of crossing." No wonder I'm anxious, she thought. It's not just me, the world is waiting with bated breath for me to settle down and procreate. It's just a date.

"Anyway, I've got to go. Speak soon. Good luck with the rest of the form," said Marise.

Chapter 15

Ger

Ger dropped by the apartment to talk business. Marise had been looking forward to showing Ger the apartment for a while now. She made them both an espresso on the coffee machine, which had been a house warming gift from Dad. She had managed to procure some organic decaffeinated coffee beans from Italy and they tasted even better than the real thing.

They laid out their papers on the table. Ger showed Marise her business plan which was pretty impressive.

"Ger, I have to tell you I've decided to come in

with you, but only on a consultancy basis. I need to be free to work on other projects if I need to or want to," said Marise.

"I thought you'd say that," said Ger, "but I would like you to guarantee me a minimum of twenty hours a week."

"Fine," said Marise. Ger showed her the company brochure and mission statement. Marise was impressed, but recommended a few minor tweaks and a less bland logo. Marise and Ger thrashed out an hourly rate.

Marise said, "Ger, fancy another coffee?"

"Actually, I took the liberty of bringing this," said Ger, producing a bottle of expensive champagne.

"You're very sure of yourself missie," said Marise, as she fetched two champagne flutes.

"You have to be," smiled Ger. "Here's to us," she said.

"To us," said Marise, thinking this was turning out

to be her year.

After Ger left, Marise looked contentedly around the apartment. She had taken a risk but she would be fine. She always was and Ger had a good head on her shoulders. She would work out of the converted spare room. It would be great. She was dreading having the goodbye conversation with her boss, but it felt right. She and Ger would be good in business together. She lay down for a while to sleep off the champagne, which had completely gone to her head.

*****

That week, she had the dreaded chat with her boss. He tried to dissuade her with more money, but her mind was made up. She had a busy few weeks in store before she left. They had a major campaign on for 'Girls Nite Out' at the Palace. She might be leaving, but she was no slouch. 'Honest days work for an honest day's pay', her Mum had always said. Besides, Dublin was tiny and she had a reputation to protect.

Chapter 16

Farewell

Timmy was holding his going away do in town. By the time Marise arrived, the rest of the crew were well oiled. She hugged Pam, who was celebrating finishing the adoption course. The home assessment was next. Jeanette had recovered from all of the form filling business and was in great form. John was alone at the end of the bar. She was surprised to see that he was doing shots. He must have fallen off the water wagon.

"Good to see you John," she said. He was merry but nice.

"You look great Marise. How have you been?" he asked jovially.

"Great… mad busy… where's Laura?" she asked nonchalantly.

"Oh, she had to go to some Pet Rescue Roadshow thing in Cork. What's your news?"

Marise spilled it all out – Anne, the trip to London, the consultancy.

"Jeez, you've had a lot on, haven't you, girl," said John. "You should have called. I miss our chats."

"Me too," blushed Marise. It was true. "So how's young love?" asked Marise. "You two are together a while now."

"Five months now," said John. "Laura's great."

"Delighted," said Marise. "I better go talk to Timmy, the man of the hour. I'm going to miss him so much. I'll catch you later," said Marise.

"Yeah, Timmy's cool," said John, totally at home with his sexuality, no homophobic him. Marise noticed anew what a great guy he was.

Timmy was knocking back the Jaegermeisters, sporting an Army Feldbluse and speaking English in a German accent, with ein bisschen deutsch thrown in for good measure. He could be so funny. Marise sidled up.

"How you doing?" asked Marise.

"Nicht schlecht Herr Specht," said Timmy.

"Well I have no idea what that means. When do you fly out?" asked Marise.

"Day after tomorrow," replied Timmy.

"So soon, no regrets?" she said, catching his eye.

"Not a one," he said.

Liar, she thought to herself. His folks probably don't even know he's going.

"That's good. You'll be back to open up an Irish branch of your famous patisserie."

"Love your work," said Timmy. "Don't look now Marise, but there's been a nice big Paddy gawping at you for the last five minutes," nodding coming from Timmy towards John.

"Oh stop, will you. He's had a few."

"I wouldn't blame him. You do look good tonight. I see you have started wearing that make-up I recommended."

That was a real compliment coming from Timmy. He was quite sparing with them.

"I'll head back to the girls," she said, as she caught Timmy eyeing up a young guy in leather pants at the bar. She had to pass John on the way back. As she passed him, he put out his hand. Unsure what to do, she shook it.

"You're a lovely woman," said John.

"Thanks. Have another drink, John," she grinned.

She couldn't help but wonder if this was a case of 'in vino veritas' or 'beer goggles' or worse. The cats away and the mouse will play. He didn't seem the type. Let him off, she thought. He has Laura and I'm meeting Paul again soon. Nice, uncomplicated Paul, just what she needed.

*****

At home later she thought of her pals. Pam was on her way to being a Mum, the home study would be over before she knew it. Timmy would befriend half of Berlin in a matter of weeks. She adored Jeanette but didn't see her enough. Sometimes, they drove her nuts but she loved her urban family.

Chapter 17

Paul

She was meeting Paul the next night and was hoping she would get out of work in time for it.

The campaign for 'Girls Nite Out' was coming together and they had stayed back late every night to get it out for sign off before she left. It had needed some tweaking, but they got there in the end. She was happy with the final version.

*****

Paul was waiting at the restaurant by the time she got there.

"Sorry I'm late. Work is mental," she said.

"No problem," he said. He was the perfect gentleman. He always held out her chair, summoned the waiter, everything. They spent most nights chatting about rugby. She tried to grasp the rules but her head was a little bit mithered. Sometimes, Marise got a sinking feeling in the pit of her stomach. He is too nice. She was afraid she would get bored. To inject a bit of life into things, she often asked him mad, often risqué questions. He answered them all dutifully, some with a raised eyebrow. He'd be really good for me like Porridge or Muesli, she thought. When all I want is Corn Flakes. Nice, safe and healthy. She'd stick at it. Nice would be a new departure for her. The not nice ones in her experience were not so fabulous either.

"Fancy a night-cap?" she heard herself say, one

night.

"I would but I've got training tomorrow. I'll call you during the week," said Paul.

"Um OK, then," she said, puzzled.

He's just not that into me, she thought. I usually have to try and beat them off. Either that or my quick-fire rounds of mad questions scare the poor devil senseless.

Chapter 18

John

One evening, she got in quite late from town. She noticed that the light on her answering machine was flashing.

'You have one new message'.

It had been left at 3am the night before. She played it back. It was John, sounding a little worse for wear.

"Marise will you give me a call when you get this?" he slurred.

It was almost ten o'clock. Was it too late? Could

she buzz him now? Then she thought he phoned me at 3am. Why the heck not. Feck it. She dialled the number.

"Hello," answered a girl's voice. It was Laura.

"Wrong number," said Marise, crashing the receiver into its cradle.

What the hell was he playing at? Why was she there? What were they at?

She resolved to date Paul with a vengeance. Eventually, she drifted off to sleep.

*****

Tomorrow was the day when Dad would find out that he was to become a grandfather in a matter of months. She couldn't believe he hadn't spotted it, Anne was heavy now. She was glad it was going to be finally out in the open. She hoped he wouldn't throw a fit.

Chapter 19

Dad

She picked up a homemade rhubarb tart, Dad's favourite, from the garage on the way to the house. We'd better sweeten him up if at all possible, she thought. She pulled into the driveway and turned the key in the lock. Dad was standing stock still by the range in the kitchen waiting for her to come.

"I suppose you have known about this all along," he said, sounding angry and hurt.

She almost dropped the tart.

"Hello yourself. I presume you mean Anne. I've

been on at her to tell you all along. I felt awful you not knowing," she said glaring at Anne.

"She didn't tell me, but I wasn't born yesterday," said Dad. "I've seen her running to the loo to be sick, morning noon and night, for absolutely ages now. Either she's with child or she's had the longest vomiting bug in history and belongs in hospital. The pair of you must think I'm a right eejit."

He looked disappointed.

"Dad I didn't want to worry you. I know you miss Mum." said Anne.

"Well, that's exactly why you should have told me. We need to stick together," said Dad. "Where's the yoke who did this to you? Gone already I suppose."

"Yes, and if he wasn't I'd have strangled him myself," said Marise.

"Spare me the details. I can only imagine what you mean by that, but he wouldn't want to feel my wrath."

"You don't even know him, either of you," said

Anne sullenly.

"That's enough out of you for one day, missie," said Dad. "Marise, get that tart into the oven. You brought it to butter me up I suppose, but I do approve," said Dad trying to sound stern.

"Don't mention rhubarb," said Anne running to the loo again. Dad and Marise rolled their eyes.

"More for us," they grinned.

Not a bad result, thought Marise. It could have been a whole lot worse. At least Anne wasn't turfed out onto the street.

Chapter 20

John

As she was pulling out of Dad's driveway, she caught a glimpse of a tall lanky fellow in the rear view mirror – John!

He had a big bag on his back and was letting himself into the family home. Don't tell me John still brings his washing home to Mammy, thought Marise.

Remembering his 'booty call' the other night, she was suddenly incensed. Who the hell did he think he was? She pulled up the handbrake on the car in the middle of the road and marched over there with the engine running. She put her finger on the doorbell and didn't take it off until he answered.

"Hey Marise, what a nice surprise," he said, his eyes twinkling. The bare-faced cheek of him standing there, all casual, as though nothing had happened.

"Eh, you left a message for me in the middle of the night asking me to phone you and when I did, your girlfriend answers. What's up with that?" she demanded to know.

"Ex-girlfriend," said John. "I moved out."

Marise hadn't known he had moved in.

"To be honest, since I spoke to you that night ages ago at Timmy's do, I realised I wasn't really in love with Laura."

"What do you mean?" she asked coyly.

"I just went along with everything, her plans and plots. I was becoming a shell, just for the sake of being with someone. It was all what she wanted. Don't get me wrong, she's a lovely girl and she was great with Rusty, but she's not for me."

"Still not with you, John," said Marise, to see if he could come out with it.

"It's you I want Marise, always have. It's always been you and only you." he said kissing her.

"Your mother will see," giggled Marise.

"No one's home," smiled John, raising one eyebrow.

"My car is in the middle of the road, engine running and don't forget this is the Northside," said Marise.

"Hey don't knock it. You might be a Southsider now but don't forget, you're from across the road."

"Drive it round the back. No one will see it there. See you in a minute," he winked. "I'll put the kettle on."

*****

They talked for hours. Marise chided him for not revealing his true feelings sooner.

"I was sure you would reject me, the lanky software geek. You seemed to have such a diverse, exciting life."

"I like lanky software geeks." said Marise.

"Marise, I've had feelings for you my whole life but thought you'd never look twice at me. Then you were engaged to that rich asshole, Richard, who broke your heart. I wanted to throttle him for cheating on you, what an eejit. I ached for you then and wanted to comfort you, but didn't want to be your rebound guy. Then we had that kiss a few years ago and it got my hopes up, but then I didn't see you for ages and it had gone cold. I reckoned you were too embarrassed to bring it up."

"Oh Richard's old news now and I was a bit embarrassed but I didn't forget the kiss," smiled Marise. "One thing concerns me though. I worry about your drinking. You don't seem to have a stop button."

"I don't. That's why I've joined this recovery group and I'm going to do their program. I reckon I'm better without it and haven't touched a drop for a while and I plan to stick at it."

"I'm glad," said Marise.

"Besides, making love is so much better sober," grinned John. "Want to find out?"

Wow! She was starting to have new found respect for this guy. They raced upstairs.

*****

They didn't surface for a day and a half, ordering in food and uncharacteristically pulling respective sickies. What the hell, life was too short and they'd missed so much already. Marise had never felt more content.

"When you meet the one you want to spend the

rest of your life with, you want that life to start today," he said in a bad Yankee drawl. "Why was I so afraid to say that before?" said John.

"Never mind, you've said it now," said Marise snuggling into him.

*****

Half-dozing, she heard her mobile beep in her jeans pocket that John had flung across his bedroom. It was a text from Paul. Crikey, she hadn't spared him a thought. She would ring him later. She'd better be nice to him, he was still a nice guy.

"By the way," said John sleepily. "Have you heard about Timmy?

"What about him?" asked Marise. She had been so wrapped up in Anne and work that she hadn't got in touch with him.

"Well, he reckons he's all settled down. He's met

'the One'."

He's a fast mover, thought Marise. He's only been gone five minutes. Meanwhile, John and I have been skirting around each other for decades and have only just got together.

"When you know, you know," said John.

"Oh, you are so cheesy," she smiled pinching his cheeks.

"Timmy is going on about a civil ceremony in July in Berlin and wants us all to come. Would you be on for it?" asked John.

"I wouldn't miss it for the world," said Marise.

"Maybe we can make it our first outing as a couple, if you'll pardon the pun."

"You're on," said Marise.

Chapter 21

The Real World

Leaving the Northside, Marise headed back to her life, her job and her apartment. She had to do it sooner or later. There were bills to be paid, plants to be watered and bins to be put out. Her answer phone was full of messages. She called Paul and let him down gently. He would be fine. He would be snapped up in no time. The girls were meeting for dinner on Wednesday night. Did she want to catch up?

She couldn't sleep that night, but she didn't care. She had lost her appetite and all the songs on the radio did make sense. Damn it, those clichés are all true, she thought, as she kept finding herself grinning inanely at nothing in particular.

*****

The girls were there by the time she arrived.

"You're looking very something Marise," said Jeanette. "This Paul guy must be doing you some good."

Marise grinned. She felt mean, but she wanted to be sure it was right before she said anything. She was almost sure about John. She was enjoying hugging it to herself for a while. She realised she had waited for John for a long time and was savouring it.

Instead she told them about Anne. They were both aghast and happy. Pam didn't bat an eyelid. She and Joe had just completed the home study and were on their way.

"How did your Dad take it?" asked Jeanette.

"Way better than expected. You know he can't stay mad for long. He spoils Anne anyway."

"She rang me earlier. He's driving her mad, telling her to take calcium in case her teeth fall out, looking into ante-natal classes and talking about baby names. It's hilarious. I warned her not to complain. Most girls would be out flat-hunting in her position. Apparently, the baby's father has been on the blower and the last time he rang, she told him to get lost. I hope she keeps her resolve."

"Folks, I have to head early tonight. I am snowed in with work for Ger, I want to get my desk cleared before I head off. Are any of you going to go to Berlin?"

Pam and Jeanette both wanted to try and make it, but weren't sure.

"It might be fun. Be nice to see Timmy again," said Jeanette.

"He works fast doesn't he?" said Pam.

"When you know, you know," said Marise grinning.

There's that look again, thought Pam happily.

"I think you have a booty call," said Jeanette.

"No at all," said Marise. "It's work."

She hated lying. She was heading over to John's place. They couldn't keep their hands off each other and she was enjoying it.

Chapter 22

Pam

A worried sounding Pam phoned Marise a week later.

"What's up, Pam?" asked Marise.

"I had to tell you in case you were falling in love. I saw Paul with another girl in town. They looked together. I just thought you should know."

"Oh that's old news. I wasn't that into him. He was nice, a bit bland, but he wasn't for me. Thanks for the heads up though".

"Oh, so you're not bothered! You just seemed so

sparkly lately. I have been worried about breaking it to you."

"No need. Don't worry. Plenty more men in the sea or is that fish? I always get that mixed up." She laughed.

"How's the adoption going?"

"Oh, you know, getting there. We are on the list for a referral from the Philippines now. We just got the Declaration."

"See, it is moving. Happy landings, you two."

Chapter 23

Berlin

John and Marise boarded the plane for Berlin. It was nice to be getting on a plane under better circumstances than before, thought Marise. The other girls couldn't make it. John and Marise were looking forward to their first mini-break as a couple. John mentioned that he might have to nip away for a breather during the festivities if the boozing atmosphere got too much.

"No bother, we can go off and explore Berlin. I have never been to Berlin before," said Marise.

She was glad they were going to be there for

Timmy. His own family weren't going to be there. His alpha-male father, Bill, had never liked Timmy's lifestyle choice and his mother was too meek to stand up to Bill or rock the boat at home. Marise realised that the real reason Timmy hammed up his homosexuality was to overcompensate for their rejection of him as a person and for what he stood for. He fobbed it off, but after a few drinks now and then it came out in the wash.

*****

Marise and John wanted to meet the husband-to-be, not to have the 'hurt him and we'll kill you conversation', it probably wouldn't translate well anyway, but to satisfy themselves that he would be in good hands with Hans (for that was his name).

*****

Thanks to their good connections in the gay community, the couple had procured a room in the Gruenderzeit Museum. A lady minister would marry them and they would have a feast fit for a king, albeit a gay king, provided by local catering friends. An usher handed them each an enormous pink chrysanthemum as they arrived.

"Good job you are secure in your masculinity," joked Marise.

"It doesn't go with my hair," joked John.

Marise felt that they really fitted together. She remembered the wedding gift, he brought the video camera. Everything was so easy with him. Privately, she thought she could do this forever with him, but didn't say it. She didn't have to.

They heard Timmy before they saw him. He was fussing and faffing in high-pitched German. He looked fabulous in a white suit. Hans looked tall, strong and handsome. He seemed very smitten with Timmy and his eyes followed him fondly round the room as Timmy hugged and chatted with everyone. Timmy came running over to air-kiss them.

As agreed, she and John said they just met on the way in.

"Sure you did?" said Timmy, with a dirty wink. "And my father is going to be the minister that marries us. Grab a seat. Have fun. It's like the UN here."

Despite Timmy's tongue-in-cheek, flamboyant nature and the fact that the ceremony was in German, they could tell it was a solemn affair. The couple meant business and it was clear the pair were serious about each other.

John and Marise partook of the buffet feast. There was an abundance of sausages, pickled gherkins, along with salads, cucumber, breads, salami and cold meats, followed by delicious pastries, banana boats and petit fours.

Judging by the gales of laughter, the speeches were hilarious, although they understood only half of it. Leaving their gift on the gift table, they said their goodbyes, content that Timmy was going to be happy. They were ready to jump into bed again.

They walked off the food and took in the sights on the way back to the hotel.

John asked, "When is Anne due?"

"God, soon," said Marise. "I must call her when I get back. She wants me at the birth, holding her hand. Maybe you and Dad can share a cigar outside, while I do the cheerleading."

"No bother," said John. "I like your old man."

Marise was glad. He'd be missing Mum and Declan.

"Listen to me plotting and planning. Next time I meet the girls, I'm going to tell them we are together. Is that alright?" she asked, testing the waters.

"It is Marise, it is," he said pulling her close, kissing her lightly on the forehead.

Chapter 24

New Arrival

Marise nipped into the homeplace on a Sunday evening. Anne looked ready to pop.

"I've another couple of days to go, but I've got my bag in the hall, just in case."

"Where's Dad?" asked Marise.

"He's upstairs on the Internet, trying to find a Dublin jersey for a newborn baby, on the Gaelic Athletic Association (GAA) website."

They both chortled with laughter. The poor kid.

She shouted up the stairs.

"Call me if anything happens."

"OK," shouted Dad. "See you soon."

*****

She had booked a week off to be around for the birth. She could do with it. Things had been full on lately. She was due to meet the girls for dinner on Saturday.

Chapter 25

The Girls

The women met in Bayoux on Baggot Street on Saturday. Pam and Jeanette were there together looking as thick as thieves.

"Hey you two, I'm starved, lets order."

They chose quickly.

"Listen, I can't keep it to myself any longer. I'm with John. He's great. I'm crazy about him."

"I told you," said Jeanette to Pam.

Pam screeched, "I knew it. I waited decades to

hear you say that."

"People are looking Pam. Stop screaming," said Jeanette.

"I don't care," she said. "Now it's my turn." Not giving a damn who heard. "I'm pregnant," she exclaimed at the top of her voice.

"We knew it would happen once you guys got your declaration," the three women shrieked excitedly. They ordered champagne and sparkling water for Pam.

"Can't to be too careful," they said.

"So you and John, eh. You are a dark horse," said Pam.

"I'm sorry, I just didn't want to jinx it or say anything until I was sure of us, I waited so long for him. My love life has been such a disaster," said Marise.

"You two belong together," said Jeanette.

"You might have something there," said Marise.

"Marise, your bag is ringing," said Pam. Marise

reached for her bag. There was a text from Dad.

"Get to Rotunda Hospital a.s.a.p. Waters broken."

"Folks I have to run. I am about to get into midwifery for my sins."

"We'll get this, go on, wish her luck from us. Text us when something happens."

"Pam, congrats again, love you guys," said Marise, as she ran to the door.

*****

In the cab, Marise texted John. He came straight back, C U THERE, BRINGING CIGARS xx.

As they crawled through the busy streets in the cab, she realised again what a great guy he was and the fact that Mum had known and liked him really helped too. To know she would have approved of him meant a lot.

One of Mum's old sayings came back to Marise as

the taxi pulled up to the kerb.

'Life is a series of comings and goings', she had always said. Ain't that the truth, thought Marise, thinking back on the year she'd had.

She shouted up at the sky, "I'll do right by Anne, Mum, don't worry. I'll do right by her."

Outside the maternity hospital the expectant mothers puffed on a cigarette in the night air and looked at Marise like she had two heads. They can talk, she thought, they can talk.

*****

Katie (named for their Mum Kathleen) was born at 2am. She weighed in at a healthy 8lb and 12oz. Dad knowledgeably put the size down to the folic acid. The real midwife, a true blue Dubliner, said she half expected to see a schoolbag come out and all.

Dad and John enjoyed their coveted cigar outside

and danced a jig up and down the street.

*****

Anne and Katie slept and Dad headed back to the house to fetch the Dublin Jersey and put a call in to Declan in Oz, to tell him he was an uncle.

John and Marise were snuggled up drinking maxpax tea from the machine in the waiting room.

"Marise," said John, "would you like one of those?"

"What, a baby?" asked Marise, surprised.

"Yes," said John.

"That'd be nice," said Marise, with a quiet smile, "that'd be nice." as she rested her head on his chest.